MAX ★★★ for ★★★ President

★ Jarrett J.★ Krosoczka ★

Alfred A. Knopf ★ New York

A special acknowledgment to
Robin Bahr Casey and Nancy Galicki
for all their dedication to student government

Library of Congress Cataloging-in-Publication Data
Krosoczka, Jarrett.
Max for president / Jarrett J. Krosoczka. – 1st ed.
p. cm.
"A Borzoi book."
SUMMARY: Max and Kelly both want to win the election for class
president, but when one of them loses, the winner finds a way to
make the loser feel better.
ISBN 0-375-82428-6 (trade) – ISBN 0-375-92428-0 (lib. bdg.)
[1. Elections–Fiction. 2. Winning and losing–Fiction.
3. Schools–Fiction.] I. Title.
PZ7.K935Max 2004
[E]–dc21   2003009947

Mrs. Antonio announced that it was time to elect a new class president.

MAX thought that he would like to be class president.

So did
KELLY.

Max made signs that said

"Max for President."

Kelly made signs, too.

Max made buttons and gave them
to all of his classmates.

So did Kelly.

Max made promises.

Kelly made promises, too.

The time came to vote. Every student could only vote for one candidate— Max or Kelly!

Max waited anxiously.

So did Kelly.

After the ballots were collected and counted, Mrs. Antonio announced the winner.

Kelly cheered.

Max didn't.

Kelly knew that she needed a good vice president to help get work done. She thought for a second and then asked . . .

And from then on, both Kelly and Max worked hard to make their school a better place.

The End